GOOD DOG

McTAVISH

GOOD DOG McTAVISH

Meg Rosoff

With illustrations by Grace Easton

onkers

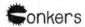

First published in 2017 in Great Britain by
Barrington Stoke Ltd
18 Walker Street, Edinburgh, EH3 7LP

www.barringtonstoke.co.uk

Reprinted 2018

A CIP catalogue record for this book is available
from the British Library upon request

ISBN: 978-1-78112-683-7

Printed and bound by CPI Group (UK) Ltd, Croydon, CR0 4YY

To the real McTavish, illustrious rogue and rascal

CONTENTS

1

McTavish Falls for the Peacheys

McTavish's decision to adopt the Peachey family was not the most sensible decision of his life. He could tell at once that they were not one of those easy families, the ones that fit effortlessly into a dog's life. He could tell they were a family with problems.

Whether they'd been traumatised early on, or were just difficult by nature, McTavish had no way of knowing. But he did know that adopting them would require patience, discipline and hard work. His logical mind told him to wait for the trouble-free family, a family with easy natures and cheerful smiles. But there was something about the Peacheys, with their sad little faces, that clinched it for him.

Oh, McTavish, he warned himself. *Are you sure you're not making a mistake? Beware! This could mean years of heartache and frustration.*

But it was already too late.

McTavish had fallen for the Peacheys.

2

Ma Peachey Gives Up

McTavish might never have met the Peacheys, if Ma Peachey hadn't decided to give up being a mother.

"I give up," she said. "No more cooking and cleaning and finding lost keys. No more keeping track of your appointments and nagging you to tidy your rooms. No more boring thankless jobs. I quit."

At first, the younger Peacheys rejoiced.

"No more healthy food!" shouted Ollie, age 12, punching the air in triumph.

"No more matriarchal oppression!" crowed Ava, age 14, looking up from the book she was reading (*The Family – A History of Despair*).

'No more nagging to get home in time for dinner,' thought Pa Peachey, though of course he would never have said such a thing out loud.

The youngest member of the family frowned.

"Mum," said Betty Peachey, "are you saying that you've ... resigned?"

Ma Peachey smiled. "Why, yes, Betty. That's an excellent way of putting it."

Betty looked concerned. "Is that legal?"

Ma Peachey shrugged. "Maybe it is, maybe it isn't. But I'm sick and tired of everyone making a mess and expecting me to clear it up. I'm done with cooking meals that get cold because no one's home to eat them. And," she said, "I'm tired of having to shout at everyone to wake up, go to bed, put away the washing, say please, say thank you, clear the dishes, stop fighting."

"But –" Betty began.

Ma Peachey ignored her. "So yes," she said, "you could say I've resigned. For now, anyway. I am taking time out to pursue peace and quiet.

From now on, the only person I am in charge of – is me."

And with that, she gave Betty a kiss on the head and went off to change into her yoga pants.

At first, none of the Peacheys really missed being told to clear the table or put the washing away. But as days turned to weeks and nobody made dinner or washed the clothes – ever – the sense of freedom wore thin.

The Peacheys ate ready meals and take-aways every night, wore the same clothes over and over, and arrived late to school and work each day. There was a great deal more squabbling and a great deal more squalor.

Betty, who was by far the most sensible member of the Peachey family (after Ma Peachey), began to feel that some sort of intervention was required. And so, one Saturday afternoon just before Easter, a family conference was held.

"Due to the loss of motherly care in our family, I am feeling lost, lonesome and lacking in love," said Betty.

Ava and Ollie sniggered, but Betty ignored them.

"I have a proposal," she said.

The rest of the Peacheys leaned forward expectantly. Across the room, Ma Peachey hummed as she worked on her lotus position.

"We could ask Ma Peachey to come back," said Betty.

Ava gasped, Ollie snorted and Pa Peachey made a tut-tut noise, that did not commit him to any opinion, but still managed to express disapproval.

Silence fell.

"Well," said Betty at last. "If we are not planning to ask Ma Peachey to come back, I have another suggestion."

Once again, the Peacheys all leaned forward to listen.

"I believe we should get a dog."

Ollie imagined a big handsome furry

creature that might help him be more

attractive to girls.

Ava imagined a large melancholy dog that

would help her look more intellectual.

Pa Peachey did not want a dog. At all. And

he said so.

A heated discussion ensued and, in the

end, the three Peachey children managed to

prevail. They would take a trip to the Dog

Home.

"Not by any means to adopt a dog," Pa

Peachey warned. "Just to browse."

"To browse?" Ollie goggled. "We're going

to *browse* lonely stray dogs doomed to spend

eternity locked up, sad and loveless, in cages?" He turned to Ava and lowered his voice to a stage whisper. "I always said there was something heartless about Pa Peachey."

Ava scowled. "Nobody browses homeless dogs. Except perhaps," she turned to glare at her father, "a sociopath."

"Never mind," said Betty. "We shall go to the Dog Home to browse, and perhaps, just perhaps, we shall find the dog of our dreams."

Ollie rolled his eyes.

Ava carefully recorded this conversation in a brown notebook. She had hopes that her book, *Memoir Of A Broken Childhood*, would sell for a large sum of money and become an international bestseller.

Ollie went back to the book he was reading, feeling (perhaps correctly) that the last thing the world needed was another book, particularly one written by his older sister.

3

Browsing

The following afternoon, the Peachey family
(minus Ma Peachey, who was working on her
warrior pose) mustered at 2 p.m. on the dot
and set off in Pa Peachey's van, which was so
full of screws and springs and gizmos and
stuff-that-might-someday-come-in-handy
that there was barely any place for an actual
human to sit.

Ava complained about the noise the van

made but no one else seemed to hear, partly because it was so noisy in the van.

Pa Peachey pulled up in front of the Cuddles Home for Unclaimed Mutts (C.H.U.M.) with a little flourish and a spin of the steering wheel.

He set the handbrake with a loud squeak, and shouted "OUT OUT OUT" over his shoulder, as if the children had been sitting in the parked van for months.

All the Peachey children were excited by the possibility that they might soon acquire a dog. Even Ava, who was famous for being hard as nails and sentimental as burnt wood.

"I can't wait to browse the poor homeless doggies," Ava whispered to Ollie.

Ollie imagined the future Peachey family dog, waiting on the other side of that door, locked in a lonely cage. The thought made him feel quite light-headed.

Betty screwed her eyes shut with longing and terror. She did not want to browse dogs. All she wanted was to choose the smartest, waggliest, most shiny-eyed of all the poor doggies in captivity, take him home and love him to bits. Maybe then the family could return to a time when Ma Peachey wasn't doing yoga, Pa Peachey wasn't angry, and Ava, Ollie and

Betty didn't feel quite so much like orphans.

Inside the Dog Home, McTavish waited quietly, not barking, not making a fuss. Just … waiting. Although he hadn't met the Peacheys, he had a dog's sixth sense about this family. He had a feeling they might be "the one".

Pa Peachey entered the Dog Home first, followed by Ollie, Ava, and Betty.

Betty was always last. Last was what happened when your parents decided to stop having children once you were born. There was no one less important to tease, annoy and torment.

Inside the Cuddles Home for Unclaimed

Mutts, a stern-looking woman in overalls greeted the Peacheys. Her tag read, *Hello. I'm Ian.*

"Hello, I'm Alice," she said.

"Ian, surely?" Ava was a stickler for accuracy in the written word.

Alice/Ian looked confused for a second, then followed the direction of eight eyes and bent her head to peer at the tag with a sigh.

"The overalls may say Ian, but please look beyond that. I am not Ian. I am Alice." She paused to scan the family with a practised eye.

The family scanned her back.

"You are here for a dog," Alice announced,

as if the thought had not occurred to the Peacheys. As if perhaps they had just stumbled into the Cuddles Home for Unclaimed Mutts on a trip to the shops, thinking it might be a good place to buy a newspaper and a carton of milk.

"Yes, we are," Betty piped up.

"No, we are most certainly *not* here for a dog," Pa Peachey said with a glare at his youngest child. "We are here to determine the lay of the land. We are not in the market for a canine at this moment in time. We are here to undertake an initial foray into the acquisition of a family pet. At some future date. Going forward."

Ollie made crazy motions with one finger

in the air by his left ear and Ava turned her

hands into quacking ducks.

"We are here," Betty said in a soft and

clear voice, "for a dog."

Despite all the time she spent complaining

about being the youngest, Betty often forgot

to notice that she held a position of great

authority in the Peachey family.

Alice held up her hand. "I am getting a

picture of this family," she said, looking down

her rather long nose and out through her

rather thick glasses. "I am getting the picture

of a family that is not always in harmony

with its desires. Is that what you would call an

accurate picture of the Peachey family?"

"Yes," said Betty.

"No," said Pa Peachey.

"Sometimes," said Ava.

"Rarely," said Ollie.

Betty sighed. "*They* are all confused. But I am not. I am here. For a dog."

From that moment on, Alice addressed all of her remarks to Betty. Who was, it is probably worth re-stating, not yet nine years old.

"Good," said Alice. "Because we have too many dogs and not enough humans to take them home and love them. Now, please sit."

Obediently, the Peachey Family sat.

4

Alice's Questions

"Now," said Alice. "I am going to ask you some questions, and I'd be grateful if only one of you answered at a time. You," she said, indicating Betty. "You seem the least lunatic member of the family, so I would like you to answer my questions. If any other person objects, please raise your paw." She paused. "I mean hand."

The Peacheys nodded.

"Excellent. Question one. Does your home have a garden?"

"Yes," said Betty. "Our home has a garden with one apple tree, uncut grass due to arguments about whose turn it is to cut it, and many many squirrels for a woofy love-dog to chase."

Alice ticked box one.

"Question two. How much exercise does a dog need each day?"

Betty thought for a moment. "I would take my dog for a walk before school each morning, and Pa Peachey would walk him again at night. Ava and Ollie could take turns walking him after school."

Alice tapped her pencil on the desk and nodded. "Question three. What are the four most important things in a dog's life? You may all confer."

They conferred, ignoring each other entirely.

"Food," said Pa Peachey.

"Water," said Ollie, who had recently learned in Biology that you could go weeks without food but only a few days without water.

"A sense of philosophical autonomy," said Ava, who always went for the existential option. Which nobody understood.

When they were done, Betty turned to

Alice with quiet dignity. "The most important thing for any dog is love. After that, it's routine. Then exercise and mental stimulation and – last of all – healthy food."

"Thank you, Betty," Alice said. "You are very wise for a young person. Particularly for a young person who has obviously been raised by wolves." She gazed sternly at Pa Peachey.

"And of course a comfy bed," Betty added. "And not being dressed up in silly clothes, like snow boots. Or little raincoats."

"All good answers. And finally, I must ask each of you if you understand the commitment dog ownership entails."

"A painfully long one," said Pa Peachey, in a mournful voice.

"It's like having another sibling," said Ava. "That bites."

"It can't be worse than a younger sister," grumbled Ollie.

Betty looked at each member of the family in turn. "I imagine that it is half way between having a friend and a baby," she said after a moment. "A dog requires a great deal of attention and care, but can also be a fine companion. A dog will love you and make you feel happy when you are lonely or low, in exchange for a life of order and kindness."

Alice jotted down some more notes. She looked up at last.

"One of you gets it," she said, tapping her pencil against the table. "And that may well be enough. I shall have to think about it. But for now, let us go and meet the dogs."

She stood and led the way into the kennels at the back. A great barking and whining started up.

"Oh my," Pa Peachey said, turning pale.

The Peachey family began to browse.

There were hairy dogs and smooth dogs, huge dogs and tiny dogs, lolling drooling dogs and neat-footed dogs as tidy as cats. Some

had stripy brown coats, others were black and white, and one was a lovely fluffy lemony sort of colour.

Ollie fell in love with a huge spotted beast that looked like a Dalmatian crossed with a dinosaur.

Pa Peachey cast admiring glances at a loyal Labrador with big amber eyes.

Ava made cooing noises at a nervous little thing that looked like a wolfhound shrunk in the wash.

Betty walked from cage to cage, her eyes sometimes filling with tears, her fists balled with determination.

After nearly an hour of watching the Peachey family browse dogs, Alice looked down and found Betty standing by her side.

"I would like to adopt every single one of these lovely doggingtons," Betty said. "But I believe I have found the one special dog for us." She took Alice's hand and led her to a quiet crate near the corner.

"Him," she said, pointing.

Alice peered at the name on the crate. She looked inside, just to make 100 per cent sure.

"McTavish," she said at last, and she smiled a small smile.

"Is that his name?" Betty asked.

Alice nodded.

Betty tilted her head and frowned. "What exactly is ... McTavish?"

"Well," said Alice. "He is quite a lot of Scottish terrier, a bit of Jack Russell, a touch of poodle, a trace of Bichon Frise ... and perhaps just a dash of" – she leaned in close to Betty, raised one eyebrow, lowered her voice and whispered, "*Chinese Spaniel.*"

Betty giggled. "McTavish," she said, and kneeled down to his level. The dog and the child looked into each other's eyes for a long moment. A very long moment.

Betty spoke at last. "I think I would

like you to come home with us," she said to McTavish in a polite voice. "That is, if you think you might like us."

McTavish looked at Betty and cocked his head to one side, thinking.

After what seemed like a very long time, he took one step forward, stuck his nose through the bars of the crate and swiped Betty's face with his tongue.

Alice opened the door to the cage, put a lead on McTavish and led him through to the Getting To Know You room. She sent Betty to collect the rest of the Peachey family.

"He's a bit short," Ollie said.

"Is it morally appropriate for one species to own another species?" Ava wondered aloud.

"*McTavish?*" Pa Peachey asked, looking worried. "Is he a foreign dog?"

Betty ignored them all. "He is a perfect dog," she said. "He is beautiful and intelligent and sensible. We will love and cherish McTavish and he will become an important and admired member of our family."

Alice took pictures on her phone, so the Peacheys would remember their first visit with the newest member of their family. The pictures showed a dog quite a bit longer than he was high, with huge triangular ears that stood up like a bat's. He had soft brown eyes, a thoughtful expression, large paws and a wiry golden coat that stuck out in all directions.

"His first owner was an old lady who became ill and could no longer care for him," Alice told them. "So he has not had a bad start in life. He is four years old and he knows his own mind. There is no question that he would make an excellent dog for this family. My question," she said, and she narrowed her eyes a little, "is whether you will make a good family for this dog."

"A dog is for life, not just for Easter," Pa Peachey warned, but no one took any notice.

McTavish looked at Betty with a serious expression. And then he bobbed his head, took a neat step into her lap, lay down and sighed.

"McTavish has spoken," said Alice.

5

Getting Ready for McTavish

Certain matters needed to be settled before McTavish took up residence with the Peacheys. Alice made a visit to the Peachey home.

"She wants to check that we're not a front for international dog smugglers," Ava said.

Ollie looked up from his book. "Is that even a thing?"

Ava shrugged. "Everything's a thing."

"We are not a front for international dog

smugglers," Ollie said to Alice. "In case you were wondering."

"I wasn't," said Alice, and handed Betty an information folder with a list of everything they would need for the safety and happiness of their new dog. "Now, where are you planning to put his bed?" she asked.

"He will sleep with me," Betty said.

"No, he will not," Alice said in a very stern voice. "A dog needs his own bed in a warm and quiet place." She looked around and settled on a snug corner under the stairs. "This corner will do perfectly. McTavish will have privacy and as much peace and quiet as he needs. He will be able to keep an eye on the comings and goings of every person in this somewhat peculiar household."

And that was that.

Alice approved the Peacheys' application to re-home McTavish and arranged to return the following morning with McTavish himself. She said she would also bring a collar and lead and a week's worth of food.

Just then, Pa Peachey emerged from his study and snatched the information folder from Betty's hand.

"A shopping list?" he exclaimed. "A shopping list for a dog? Whatever next? Ballet lessons? Summer camp?"

Betty opened her mouth to explain but Pa Peachey waved for silence.

"A bed," he exclaimed. "A bed for a dog? What nonsense. Why not a dog automobile? Or a dog aeroplane? Any animal worth his salt would make his own bed. He'd burrow down under the house, carry in straw and moss and live there in a nest. That's what dogs did in my day."

The three children stared at him blankly.

"In your day," Ollie said, "dinosaurs roamed the earth."

Pa Peachey ignored him. "And what's this? Dog food? He's a predator, goddamn it. Send the lazy so-and-so out to hunt for his own food."

Betty stepped forward. "Pa," she said, "McTavish is not a predator. He is a house dog, a companion and friend. A domestic animal. He would require years of training to learn to fend for himself. He might even take to preying upon cats or small children. Which would soon present other problems."

Betty had a good line in dealing with Pa Peachey that the two older children admired greatly.

"Pfft," Pa Peachey said, which was his way of backing down. "What else am I being fleeced for?" He scanned the list and handed it back to Betty. "This whole dog nonsense is nothing but a, a, a ..." Unable to think of an appropriate word to end the sentence, he left the room.

Betty disappeared into the loft and returned with a grubby flannel sleeping bag left over from Ava's Girl Guide days and an old grey wool blanket. She stuffed the sleeping bag and the blanket into the washing machine and switched it on. When both were clean and dry, she sat down in front of the TV with a large needle and a ball of red yarn from her mother's knitting basket. With a pair of scissors, she trimmed the blanket into one large rectangle. Then with big red stitches, she began to sew the edges together while

watching a documentary about the intelligence of starfish.

"Hello, dear," Ma Peachey said, as she passed through the house on her way to her evening yoga class.

"Hello, Ma," said Betty. "We have adopted a dog. His name is McTavish and I think you will like him."

"How nice," said Ma Peachey. "But who is planning to walk and feed and care for McTavish?"

"We are," said Betty, and returned to her sewing.

Ma Peachey picked up her yoga bag and smiled a small smile.

"Excellent," she said to no one in particular.

Once Betty had sewn the blanket into a pocket, she stuffed the sleeping bag inside, punched it around, sewed up the open side and settled the warm and fluffy new bed into the corner under the stairs.

"There," she said, with satisfaction. "McTavish doggity-dog will love this."

And how could he not? It was cosy and squashy and clean, it was grey wool with a bold red blanket stitch around the edges, and even Ava was tempted to sneak into the corner and settle down for a little read.

But she didn't. Because Betty would have squawked.

6

McTavish Comes Home

McTavish made himself at home at once.

He discovered his new bed, stamped it down and dug around with his paws until the sleeping bag stuffing shifted to his exact specifications. Then he turned around four times and settled with his rump towards the corner and his head pointed out at the rest of the house.

As Alice had predicted, it was a good spot. It allowed McTavish to monitor who was upstairs and who was down, who was coming in the front door and who was going out the back. He could see who was skulking in the kitchen looking for leftovers – and who was prowling aimlessly, seeking a fight.

That person was nearly always Pa Peachey.

Pa Peachey had not been happy of late.

Although not a cheerful baby and quite a pessimistic child, Pa Peachey's bad temper took a serious turn when Ma Peachey announced her latest plan.

"I am going to India to explore my spiritual self. With my new yoga teacher, Pradeep," she said.

Pa Peachey frowned. Pradeep was a very

handsome young man, with flexible shoulders, firm thighs and a serene expression.

Ollie, Ava and Betty thought Pradeep looked very calm and could understand why Ma Peachey found him restful after so many years with Pa Peachey.

Pa Peachey may have been gloomy, but he was a passionate man. He felt passionate about most subjects, including family, the history of the lawn mower and whether or not to get a dog. So when Ma Peachey said she was going away with Pradeep, the serene and handsome yoga teacher, he went a bit – well, there's no other word for it, he went a bit loopy.

He shouted. He stomped around. He criticised the children and tried to kick the dog.

While Pa Peachey went loopy, Ma Peachey practised yoga. Ollie, Ava and Betty tried to stay out of sight. Chaos reigned in the Peachey household. Chaos, that is, in the form of arguments, bad temper and a general mood of gloom.

This was how McTavish found things when he first arrived at his new home. He observed the Peacheys in silence, needing to know what sort of family he had chosen, and what his role in that family would be.

In case you are still not certain, McTavish

was not one of those ball-chasing, hole-digging dogs you meet so often in books. McTavish was more of a psychological mastermind. He liked to organise people, to fix situations that were not to his liking. And to arrange the world in a way that made it most comfortable for himself.

McTavish felt a strong bond with the younger Peacheys (particularly, of course, with Betty), but he had some very definite concerns about the older Peacheys.

All that first day, he lay on his bed, not barking to go out, not begging for food or asking to play ball. Instead, he observed.

Here is what he observed.

He observed that Pa Peachey was not a bad person, but he had a cranky, resentful side.

He observed that Ma Peachey had turned to yoga to escape from her family, and that she would almost certainly return some day. But perhaps one reason she needed to escape was that she had become fed up with Pa Peachey's cranky, resentful side.

McTavish also observed that despite the Peachey children's niceness, intelligence and good manners, they had many failings. For instance, they failed to pick up after themselves and they failed to take much notice of anyone else in the family.

McTavish observed that the one member of the family who was without any great failings, was Betty. He observed Betty with a strange sort of pride. Betty was, after all, his main person in the family. And a most superior sort of person she was, for a human.

However, even an ordinary run-of-the-mill dog (and McTavish was no ordinary dog) could see that the Peachey family had a problem. And it was clear that the family problem needed to be solved if McTavish was to get any peace and quiet.

So he set to work.

7

The Peachey Problem

"Where are the keys?" Pa Peachey thundered.

"Who's stolen my homework?" Ava Peachey shouted.

"We're out of milk," moaned Ollie Peachey.

It was 9 a.m. and nearly every member of the Peachey family was late. Late for breakfast, late for school, just plain late.

In addition, the Peachey kitchen was so cluttered with papers and books and discarded items of clothing that it was impossible to navigate from table to fridge, much less to prepare meals there. Breakfast was a disaster, lunch impossible, and dinner barely deserved a mention.

Pa Peachey had taken to buying microwave meals that required no saucepans and almost no cleaning up. Which was a success. Except that none of the Peacheys actually liked microwave meals.

Ma Peachey was too busy meditating to care what the family ate for dinner. She lived on brown rice and clean thoughts.

"These meals are really very convenient,"

Pa Peachey said. He did not dwell on the fact that they tasted horrible. They were full of sugar and salt and chemicals that made your head feel bad and your wallet feel empty. Not to mention all the plastic, foil and guilt about the destruction of the rainforest.

McTavish began to wonder if anyone in the Peachey family even knew how to cook. It wasn't so much that he hated the dry food Alice brought from the Dog Home, but he would have much preferred a nice lamb bone now and again with some leftover vegetables and bacon rind.

Or at the very least, a tasty spinach and goat cheese omelette.

"Where are my house keys?" Pa Peachey shouted for the 12th time that morning. "No one will get to school if I can't find my keys."

"I don't care about your keys," Ava wailed. "Why are there no clean knickers? I'm going to be late *again*."

"*Ohmmmmm*," Ma Peachey chanted, on her way to inner peace.

It was obvious why no one could find anything.

The clean and dirty laundry sat together in a tangled mess on a large armchair formerly used for sitting. Shoes (never in pairs) seemed to stray around the house at random, turning up in the most unexpected places – the back seat of the car, the bottom drawer of Pa Peachey's desk, the broom cupboard. Keys wandered out of pockets and disappeared for ever.

The Peachey household was a mess.

McTavish laid his head on his front paws and gazed at the ceiling. He knew that humans were an inferior race, but their foolishness never ceased to amaze him.

Why? he thought. *Why can't they think for themselves?*

Any dog worth his salt could organise his way into a family. The key was to arrange regular meals and walks and concentrate on snoozing most of the day while the humans did all the work and earned the money to pay for it. Really clever dogs also sometimes got pigs' ears and trips to the country, and no one made them pay for the petrol or the B&B.

In contrast, moderately clever humans worked at jobs they hated with bosses they couldn't stand, slaving long hours and becoming more and more unhappy. Once or twice a year, they went away for a week to the seaside where it always rained.

Sometimes McTavish felt a little sorry for humans. There was no question at all that even a run-of-the-mill dog had a better life than a moderately clever human, though every human McTavish had ever met considered himself vastly superior to all other members of the animal kingdom.

Humans were puzzlingly dim.

McTavish sighed. There was so much work to do.

8

Plan A

Betty was at the end of her tether.

She hated seeing her father unhappy. She hated ready-meals. She hated all the mess in the house. She hated the fact that everyone overslept and was late for school. And she hated the fact that her mother had changed – from a fairly ordinary mother with a proper job who cooked and cleaned and got everyone out of bed and to school at the right time, to the opposite of all that.

Betty's mother had quite an important job as an accountant. These days, she still went to work, but spent all her spare time meditating, perfecting the lotus in tripod position or her handstand scorpion. And planning her trip to India with Pradeep.

'A mother might want to abandon her family to seek inner peace,' Betty thought, 'but it's not very nice for the family.'

Mothers were meant to dedicate themselves to keeping order and good cheer, while having their own careers and reminding the father of the house which child's birthday was next week and when the dishwasher needed unloading.

Weren't they?

Betty thought a great deal about this subject.

'What *is* the purpose of a mother?' she wondered.

The fact that family life was going downhill since Ma Peachey stopped making it her first priority suggested that mothers held some sort of key to family happiness. Yes, fathers were important, but mothers were fundamental.

Now, Betty may have been not quite nine years old, but she considered herself a feminist. She did not like the idea that the Peacheys were incapable of preparing decent meals and keeping the house clean while Ma Peachey sought inner peace.

Surely they could exist in the absence of a full-time mother?

Betty discussed the situation with McTavish. She and McTavish went on long walks together. They sat on McTavish's bed and talked, or at least Betty talked, while McTavish listened. Betty and McTavish had remarkably similar temperaments given that they came from completely different species. They both required harmony and order. And so, they became allies.

Now, if you think that dogs mostly dream of juicy bones and comfy beds, I can tell you that this is not true. McTavish spent a great deal of his time coming up with plans. After only a few days with the Peacheys, and after consulting with Betty, a really excellent plan began to form in his head.

He called it Plan A.

The first element of Plan A required McTavish to collect all the discarded jumpers and blankets and socks and pillows in the house, and drag them into his corner under the stairs. He piled them carefully in and around his bed and stamped them down to make a sort of platform.

The house looked instantly tidier and McTavish was much more comfortable. So was Betty, who could now sit under the stairs with McTavish without having to push him over to make room for her on his bed. With all these nice jumpers and pillows, both Betty and McTavish could lie on their backs and stretch their legs, a position which everyone knows is excellent for thinking.

Betty and McTavish were delighted with Plan A. But not everyone in the family agreed.

Ava went on a rampage, claiming that her best jumpers had disappeared from under the bed, which is where she usually kept them.

Ollie complained that there were no clean towels in the damp pile under the sink in the bathroom. Which was where he usually kept them.

Pa Peachey could not find two socks that matched in the huge heap of dirty clothes near the laundry basket. And if he did find two that matched, they usually smelled like old feet. Because nobody had washed them.

'That's Ma Peachey's job,' Pa Peachey thought, despite the fact that it no longer was.

The laundry pile was a particular triumph for McTavish. It included many soft and comfortable things to lie on and even one very fine Scottish cashmere cardigan.

McTavish was very fond of Scottish cashmere.

Now that he'd implemented Plan A,
McTavish waited for the result.

He waited.

And he waited.

And he waited.

But nothing happened.

Nothing at all.

Not a single thing.

Not even one teensy tiny thing.

Nothing.

And so he sighed, and began to think
again, and after some time, McTavish came up
with Plan B.

9

Plan B

Plan B consisted of chewing. McTavish chewed papers. He chewed boxes. He chewed gloves. But best of all, he chewed shoes. He focused most of his energy on chewing shoes.

Here's how he decided which shoes to chew.

He waited until everyone in the house had gone off to work or school, and then he scouted around looking for shoes that were not where they should be. Although chewing shoes is not a very nice habit for a dog, it must be said in his defence that he only chewed shoes that were out of place.

McTavish did not enter cupboards to find shoes. He did not touch shoes that were carefully lined up by any Peachey's bedside (though to be fair, there were no such shoes). Had anyone left a tidy line of shoes by the front door, he would not have chewed them.

But all other shoes – or trainers or slippers or boots – were fair game, particularly if one shoe was left lying at a great distance from its fellow shoe.

Let us pause here. It might be that you are beginning to think of McTavish as a bad and lazy dog. But on that point you would be entirely wrong. Because chewing shoes is no job for a lazy dog. Chewing shoes is very hard work.

If you are not convinced that destroying an entire leather shoe with nothing but your teeth is hard work, perhaps you should try it some time and see how it goes. Chances are you will begin to see what a difficult task McTavish set out to accomplish.

In short, shoe-chewing is not a job for the faint of heart.

But McTavish was not a faint-hearted dog.
He was a dog of great courage and purpose,
and he was determined to make a success of
Plan B.

On the third day of McTavish's shoe-
chewing campaign, Alice phoned the Peachey
family to see how they were getting on with
their new dog.

"How is dear sweet adorable McTavish?"
Alice asked. "I can tell you that I had a great
deal of trouble giving up that dog for adoption.
I was very tempted to keep him for myself."

"*Dear* McTavish?" Pa Peachey snorted.
"That dog is a monster."

Meg Rosoff

"*Sweet* McTavish?" Ava Peachey exclaimed. "That dog is a rampant destroyer of shoes and an incorrigible collector of clothing."

"*Adorable* McTavish?" Ollie Peachey grumbled. "He will not look adorable when I kick him all the way to Mars for eating my favourite trainers and dragging my best clothes into his bed."

"*Ohhhmmmm*," hummed Ma Peachey.

Betty Peachey took hold of the phone. "McTavish is doing very well, thank you, Alice. He is clever, affectionate, well-organised and intelligent. In addition, I have a strong feeling that McTavish is a dog with a plan." Betty lowered her voice and crawled into the cupboard under the stairs for privacy. "And this family, Alice, is in desperate need of a plan."

At the other end of the phone, Alice sighed. "I fear you are correct, Betty. I suspected problems when I first met the Peachey family. But I have faith in McTavish. He has your best interests at heart, and if any dog can improve the muddled mess that is the Peachey family, it's McTavish."

"Yes," said Betty. "I am quite sure he is carrying out a plan as we speak, although I am not sure what it is."

"We must have faith."

"I have faith," said Betty. "He is a very good dog."

"Indeed he is," Alice said.

"Goodbye, Alice."

"Goodbye, Betty."

Betty emerged from the cupboard under the stairs to find the Peachey family standing in a semi-circle, staring at her. Ollie held on tight to McTavish, his fingers round the dog's tartan collar.

"We need a family meeting," Pa Peachey said.

"Indeed we do," Ollie chimed in.

"A meeting," Ava added. "Now."

Pa Peachey opened the meeting.

"I am sorry to say," he said, "but this dog, this so-called *McTavish*, is turning out to be nothing short of a disaster. He behaves like a hooligan, stealing our best clothes and dragging them into his lair."

"His 'lair'?" Betty said. "McTavish is not a dragon."

"He might as well be," Pa Peachey said. "He has destroyed the very fabric of our family."

"He has destroyed the very fabric of my jeans," Ava pointed out with a frown. McTavish had not, in fact, destroyed her jeans. He had merely added them to his comfy nest under

the stairs, and did not offer to move when Ava
came searching for them.

"If you had not left them on the floor
by the laundry basket –" Betty began, but Pa
Peachey interrupted.

"Ollie?" he said, pointing pointedly at his
older son. "Every member of the family must
testify."

Betty rolled her eyes. "Is this the Supreme
Court?" she asked. "Is this the War Crimes
Commission?"

"Well," said Ollie. "McTavish has behaved
badly. That is undeniable."

"I deny it entirely," Betty said. "*We* have

behaved badly. We have left our clothes all over the floor, all over the kitchen, all over the stairs and the bathroom and every square inch of the house. No one can find anything in this house because of the chaos. It has spread to every room like some horrible creeping menace."

Ava glared at Betty. "The creeping menace is that dog of yours."

"McTavish does not creep," Betty said. "And he is not a menace."

Pa Peachey made a steeple of his fingers and tapped them together. Then he stood and cleared his throat. "We have heard from all parties," he said. "And it is clear that we have a bad and disruptive animal on our hands. I, however, have an idea."

The children all leaned forward. This was the first time Pa Peachey had come up with an idea in as long as any of them could remember.

In the corner of the room, Ma Peachey practised her looping cobra pose.

"I suggest," Pa Peachey said, "that from now on, we all put our clothes away in their proper places. I propose that we put laundry in the laundry basket. I propose that one person each week shall be assigned to sort, wash and fold the laundry, and that each family member shall be responsible for returning his or her own clothes to his or her own room."

The children stared at him open-mouthed.

"As for shoes," he said, "it would be a very good idea to take them off when entering the house. And leave them in tidy pairs on the shoe rack by the front door." Pa Peachey said this in a calm tone of voice with no trace of anger. When he finished speaking, he sat down.

Ava and Ollie goggled at their father.

"I think that is a most wonderful and excellent idea," Betty said.

In the corner of the room, Ma Peachey executed a near-perfect looping cobra, which may or may not be what caused her to smile.

In his basket under the stairs, McTavish shut his eyes and sighed a contented sigh.

10

Plan C

A hideous mess was no longer the first thing you saw upon entering the Peachey household. Shoes sat in tidy pairs by the front door. Clothes were neatly folded and put away in drawers. Car keys, homework and trainers no longer disappeared under piles of rubbish.

The Peachey home seemed to breathe more easily without its burden of chaos. Family life improved. But not all their problems were solved.

In the old days before yoga, Ma Peachey had referred to herself – sometimes in jest – as the family alarm clock. She woke every morning at 6.30, put on the coffee, made breakfast, and only then shouted for everyone to wake up. Which they sometimes did, and sometimes didn't.

Nowadays, she woke at 6.15 a.m., prepared herself a cup of hot water and ginger to stimulate and cleanse the system and practised yoga for an hour and a half. Then she changed out of her yoga clothes, showered, applied lipstick and made herself (herself *only*) a bowl of rough porridge with anti-oxidant berries. She left the house at 8.15 on the dot.

Everyone else overslept.

Even when the alarm clock rang loud enough to wake the dead, most of the Peacheys slept on. Not Betty, who liked to use the early mornings to read a book. Not Ma Peachey, who liked to use early mornings to practise her crane pose. But everyone else.

Mornings for Ollie and Ava went like this.

Pa Peachey woke up late and shouted for Ollie and Ava to hurry. But they did not hurry. Ollie often had a bath with his headphones on, so he wouldn't hear Ava pounding on the bathroom door. Ava sometimes got distracted by Instagram. Everyone skipped breakfast while Pa Peachey slopped coffee onto the floor and sometimes down the front of his suit, which led to more shouting. It was not a pleasant start to the day.

After one particularly shouty Monday, on which all three children were late to school and Pa Peachey sloshed coffee everywhere, McTavish took the family time-keeping into his own four paws.

He referred to this privately as Plan C.

Dogs are not given nearly enough credit for their time-keeping abilities. If you doubt your dog's ability to tell the time, here's a test. Take him (or her) out for a walk every day at exactly the same time. Do this for a week or two, and then one day, when walk time comes around, do not bother getting up from whatever you are doing to fetch the lead.

What do you suppose will happen?

If you own a dog, you know what will happen.

Your dog will come running with a hurt and puzzled look on its face. First, it will stare at you. If staring does not prove effective, it will begin to whine. If staring and whining do not prove effective, your dog will stand by the door, pacing back and forth like a caged beast. He might fetch his lead and drop it noisily onto the floor. Or put a paw in your lap with an insistent expression that says, "Walk. Now."

Your dog will begin this show of impatience within a minute or two of when you normally walk it. Because dogs are very good at telling the time. They do it without a clock or a watch or a mobile phone.

Really, they do.

So what did McTavish do?

He set his own alarm clock. The one in his head.

At 7 a.m. on the dot, he began barking to go out. He barked and barked, until one member of the family eventually got up, cursing and muttering, to let him out into the garden. That family member nearly always returned at once to bed, and thence to sleep.

McTavish waited just long enough for this to happen, and then began barking to come back in.

At this point, a muttering cursing person – sometimes the same one, sometimes not – would get out of bed and let him back in, returning to bed while McTavish raced from room to room yapping and pawing and licking and wagging and generally making a complete nuisance of himself until every member of the muttering cursing Peachey family was wide awake.

For a medium-sized dog with fairly short

legs, McTavish had a very impressive bark.
Once he began to bark, it became impossible to
stay in bed, so that eventually the Peacheys got
up, still muttering and grumbling. Meanwhile,
McTavish enjoyed an invigorating game of
dodge the slipper, dodge the pillow and dodge
the books that were thrown at him in a spirit
of deep resentment.

Only Betty got out of bed quietly and
calmly, had a shower, got dressed and went
downstairs to prepare breakfast.

For the first few days, McTavish kept up the
pressure until it was time to leave for school.

He growled when Ollie or Ava tried to go

back to bed. He yapped and snapped when they lingered over breakfast. At precisely 7.55 a.m., he made a last circuit of the kitchen, where Ollie would be eating toast and Ava would be reading philosophy, where Pa Peachey would be fussing and faffing and Betty would be putting on her coat.

McTavish began howling at one minute to eight, so Betty knew it was time to fetch the lead and attach it to his collar. If any member of the family was not ready to leave the house by eight o'clock, McTavish turned up the volume of his howl so that they had no choice but to leave the house. Or go mad.

Ollie missed lying in bed until one minute to eight and arriving at school without breakfast, without his school books and without most of his school uniform.

Ava occasionally used the early mornings to catch up on her reading of *Great Philosophical Riddles of the Western World*. She had no desire to get out of bed even when an insistent dog pulled her duvet to the floor. She hissed threats at McTavish, such as, "I am going to call the Dog Squad. They will come and take you away."

"I didn't know we were getting an alarm clock," Pa Peachey said, in a gloomy tone of voice. "I thought we were getting a dog."

"He *is* a dog," Betty said. "A dog who keeps time."

"He is SO annoying," said Ollie, glaring at McTavish.

"I *like* lying in bed," Ava said. "Much more than I like going to school."

Not one single member of the family (except for Betty and Ma Peachey) appreciated the McTavish alarm clock.

"That dog," Pa Peachey said, "is an infernal nuisance and I'm going to look into sending him back to the Dog Home."

But for the first time in months, all the Peacheys who needed to be out of the house at eight o'clock, were out of the house at eight o'clock.

McTavish's people-training technique worked so well, that after the first week he was able stop all his nagging, all his barking and howling. He had only to bark sharply once, at seven o'clock, and again at 7.30 to muster the Peacheys down for breakfast. At five minutes to eight, everyone was ready to go. Except for Ma Peachey, who practised her flying pigeon pose until 8.05, and left for work in a calm state of mind at 8.15.

Miraculously, mornings became almost civilised. And not one of the Peacheys was late to school or work ever again.

11

The Peacheys Eat Pizza

It was a Saturday.

Ma Peachey had been practising her
dancing warrior all day and it was nearly time
for supper with no sign of anything to eat.

Betty looked thoughtful and Ava broke
off from her writing to shout (at no one in
particular), "Is there anything for supper or
shall we all just starve?"

Ollie muttered that starvation was definitely on the menu.

At just that moment, Pa Peachey came in from the garden. He looked around, taking in the general tidiness of the house. For the first time in days, he smiled.

Ollie, Ava and Betty greeted him.

"There's nothing in the fridge," Ava moaned.

"I've got an exam on Monday and I'm starving!" Ollie kicked the wall.

"We could send out for pizza. Again," Betty said, with a despondent air. Even pizza lost its appeal after the 12th night in a row. "Maybe there's a flavour we haven't tried yet."

"There isn't," Ollie said, kicking the wall again.

The Peacheys sent out for pizza and sat around the table nibbling it listlessly. McTavish watched them eat. He was far too well-mannered to beg at the table, but when Ollie's unfinished slice found its way into McTavish's bowl, it was only polite of him to taste it.

McTavish licked the edge and walked away. Even he was sick of pizza.

Betty watched with a frown. McTavish hadn't eaten his dinner the night before. And now that she thought about it, he hadn't touched his breakfast this morning.

"Ava? Ollie? Has anyone been feeding McTavish on the sly?" asked Betty.

Ava and Ollie shook their heads.

Betty phoned Alice.

"Well," said Alice, sounding concerned, "I've never known McTavish to refuse food before. He's always been a good eater. But perhaps he's got a stomach bug. Try not feeding him at all tomorrow, but leave him plenty of fresh water. Twenty-four hours without food should settle his stomach."

Betty didn't feed him the following day.

The day after, she tried again.

But McTavish just sniffed his food and went back to bed.

She called Alice again. "He hasn't eaten in three days, Alice. Shall we take him to the vet?"

"Does he have any other symptoms? Loose bowels? Vomiting? Is he enjoying his walk? Does he seem cold? Or hot? Is he sleeping more than usual?"

Betty thought for a moment. "Not really, no, no, yes, no, no, no."

"Well," Alice said, "I suggest you try one more thing before taking him to the vet. It's the age-old cure for dogs who are off their food. Steamed chicken and rice."

"Steamed chicken and rice? That's all?" Betty said.

"That's all. It's simple and healthy and if he's recovering from a bug, it won't upset him. If he eats the chicken and rice, then a few days later you can add some lightly steamed vegetables. Nothing too strong – peas, maybe, a little spinach or some sweet potato."

Betty put down the phone, took some money out of her piggy bank, put on her coat and went out to the shops. She bought some very nice plump chicken breasts and a packet of rice, brought it home, followed the instructions on the rice and looked up a recipe for poached chicken breasts on the internet.

After ten minutes, Ollie and Ava gravitated to

the kitchen, like iron filings drawn to a magnet.

"What's that lovely smell?" Ollie asked.

Ava pulled the lid off the pan with the lightly poached chicken breasts in it, closed her eyes and sniffed.

"Mmm," she said. "Proper food at last!"

Betty took the lid from Ava's hand and replaced it. "It's for McTavish," she said. "He's not well and I'm making him a special dinner."

Pa Peachey arrived home from work at just that moment.

"What's that delicious smell?" he called from the hall. "Don't tell me we're not having pizza tonight? That *is* good news!"

Betty informed him that the meal was for McTavish.

For a miserable moment the entire family stood in the kitchen smelling the delicious smell of poached chicken and rice.

Then Ollie sighed, picked up the phone and ordered pizza. Again.

"So it has come to this," Pa Peachey sighed. "The animal eats like royalty while we scrabble about in the trash heap for scraps like vermin. McTavish is king and we? We are nothing but rats."

Everyone ignored him.

Betty checked the chicken for doneness,

prodded the rice with a fork, chopped the food into bite-size pieces, poured some of the stock into the bowl, allowed it to cool, and placed it on the floor.

"McTavish," she called softly. "Come and have something to eat."

It is worth noting that dogs have a sense of smell at least a thousand times better than humans. At Betty's call, McTavish stood up, approached his bowl, sniffed it, took a small bite, chewed for a moment and then downed the rest of the meal in a flash.

"Good boy, McTavish!" Betty said, relieved.

"Good boy? Good boy?" Pa Peachey was outraged. "Who wouldn't be a good boy, eating tender chicken breasts while the rest of us gnaw crusts with our gruel?"

No one spoke a word during their usual dinner of take-away pizza, except for Pa Peachey, who occasionally muttered something about rats.

The next day, Betty poached more chicken. Only this time, she added peas, a little spinach and some sweet potato. Once again, the Peacheys huddled round the kitchen, craning their necks and sniffing the delicious aroma of poached chicken, rice and fresh vegetables.

To everyone's relief, McTavish gulped down his whole dinner. He even licked the bowl afterwards, in case he might have missed something. The entire Peachey family sighed when he finished. They were quiet, each thinking how nice it would be to have a lovely chicken dinner with vegetables prepared at home in their very own kitchen.

If only Ma Peachey would stop practising her cow-face pose, her star pose and her lizard lunge, and return to cooking.

For a long moment, nobody spoke. At last, Betty broke the silence.

"What if," she began.

Everyone leaned forward, wondering what on earth she would say next.

"What if," she went on, "we were to borrow some of McTavish's food and cook a special dinner tonight?"

"Dog food?" gasped Pa Peachey. "Oh, that *is* rich. It's not enough that we're reduced to sifting through the rubbish for crumbs and crusts, for leftovers and leavings, for scrapings and scraps. Now we're reduced to eating dog food." He clasped a hand to his forehead. "Thank goodness my sainted parents didn't live to see this day."

"Granny and Grandad are alive and well," Betty said, with a stern look. "And the food McTavish has been eating is not dog food. It is food. Good food. It is much nicer than the food we've been eating every night. It is healthy and delicious. And although it is more expensive than dog food, it is, in fact ..." She pulled out a notebook and pencil, scribbled some sums and then looked up. "It is definitely cheaper than pizza."

The Peacheys gasped as one. "Cheaper than pizza?"

"And better," said Betty. "Healthier and more delicious."

"But what about Ma Peachey?" Ollie asked. "Isn't she meant to cook our dinner?"

"Ma Peachey has decided to seek inner

peace in India with Pradeep," Betty said. "And to cook no more. So perhaps we should just get on with cooking for ourselves, rather than night after night eating food we don't like."

The Peacheys all stared at Betty as if she had just discovered a cure for the common cold.

"Really?" said Ava. "*Us cook?* Is that even possible?"

"Us?" said Ollie. "*Us cook?* Is that even legal?"

"Yes," said Betty. "I believe it is possible. And legal."

"Well, what are we waiting for?" Ollie was already sprinting to the fridge.

That night, the Peacheys all helped with the cooking. They pan-fried chicken breasts in lemon juice and olive oil and served them on a bed of steamed spinach and rice, with a side of roasted sweet potato sprinkled with pumpkin seeds. It was the most delicious meal any of them could remember eating in as long as any of them could remember.

From his watch post under the stairs, McTavish observed the goings-on through half-closed eyes. If you hadn't known he was a dog, you might have thought that the expression on his face was a teensy bit smug.

12

The Peacheys Pitch In

For the next ten days, the Peacheys all pitched in to do the shopping, the cooking and the clearing up.

They discovered that cooking is not difficult. It is simpler than learning to play professional snooker or becoming a ballerina or flying a jumbo jet. Ollie, in particular, was stunned at how easy it was to follow a recipe.

"Why, this is far easier than studying

for a chemistry exam," he said, with an air of astonishment. "And it's even easier now than it was last week."

Ava was chopping onions, wearing an old diving mask they had bought for a seaside holiday many years ago.

"I rather like chopping," she said. "It's a great deal less difficult than reading French philosophy."

Betty stood at the stove, stirring and tasting, and consulting the recipe.

When the three Peachey children worked together, they could produce an excellent, healthy meal in not much more than half an hour.

They made sausages and mash with steamed green beans in no time at all. It was so delicious, Ava felt like fainting.

They made spaghetti Bolognese in less time than it took to study a take-away menu and decide what to eat.

They made vegetable soup and roast chicken.

They made pumpkin curry and rice.

They attempted to outdo each other with the ease and deliciousness of their recipes.

Each night Pa Peachey came home in a better mood than the night before. The meals that greeted him were tasty and tempting.

They were beautifully prepared and presented.

"What's this?" Pa Peachey demanded one night, about a meal so beautiful and tempting, he might have put it on his Facebook page. If he'd had one.

"It is fish pie," said Betty. "I made the pastry, which is far simpler than it looks. Then I added some fish, carrots and frozen peas, plus a very simple sauce and *voila*!" She held out the golden steaming pie so the whole family could say *Ooh!*

The whole family said *Ooh!*

Even Ma Peachey looked up from her flying dolphin pose to say *Ooh!*

Betty served up her fish pie and smiled modestly as every member of the family clapped her on the back and told her that she was an amazing cook for a not-quite-nine-year-old, or even for an actual person, and that her fish pie tasted even better than it looked.

Only Ollie lowered the tone by saying that he wished they had made chocolate cake for pudding.

"Maybe tomorrow," Betty said. And, still smiling, she scraped the leftovers (though there weren't many) into McTavish's bowl. McTavish tasted the fish pie and turned to Betty.

"*Ooh!*" he woofed.

Plan C, McTavish thought, *has been an excellent plan*. This was the best fish pie he'd ever eaten. Possibly the best fish pie of all time.

He licked his chops and toddled back to bed feeling very satisfied with his life. And very proud of his Peacheys.

13

A Most Impressive Dog

The day after the fish pie triumph, Ma Peachey woke up very early. She got out of bed, showered, dressed and padded down to the kitchen.

"Hello, McTavish," she said to McTavish.

McTavish heaved himself out of a peaceful slumber to greet her, stretching into a textbook example of the downward dog pose.

Ma Peachey bent down and gazed into his eyes. "You don't think I've noticed," she whispered. "But I have. You are quite an impressive dog, and I have a great deal to thank you for."

McTavish smiled, in the way that dogs smile, with a soft little woof and a squirmy sort of wriggle.

Ma Peachey kissed McTavish on the top of his head and rose to her feet. But she didn't unroll her yoga mat. She didn't perform her salutation to the sun pose. She didn't click "buy" on the flights to India in her online shopping basket.

Instead, she went to the kitchen and began to take out the ingredients for chocolate cake.

Ma Peachey hummed as she beat the sugar and butter. She whistled as she folded in eggs, flour, baking powder and melted chocolate. An hour later, she positively broke into song as she traced a large "9" on the finished cake along with the words "Happy Birthday Betty".

McTavish went back to bed with a contented sigh. *Humans make excellent pets*, he thought. When you took on a rescue family, it often took some weeks for them to settle, but he was glad he'd decided to adopt the Peacheys.

As with most humans, all they'd needed was training, combined with common sense and discipline. Despite their early lack of promise, McTavish felt certain that the Peacheys would turn out fine. With a little more work and a consistent routine, they would turn out to be a most satisfactory family after all.

About Blue Cross

McTavish is a fictional rescue dog, but in real life not all homeless dogs end up with a nice family like the Peacheys. That's why all the royalties from this book will go to the animal charity, Blue Cross, which – since 1897 – has worked tirelessly to give abandoned, unwanted, ill or injured pets a healthy life and a happy home. The charity's animal hospitals, veterinary clinics and rehoming services care for many thousands of dogs, cats, small pets and horses in need. It receives no government funding and relies on every single pound donated by its kind supporters to help pets in need. To find out more about Blue Cross's vital, often life-saving, work visit bluecross.org.uk.

If you or your family are thinking of getting a dog – or a cat or a pony! – why not adopt one of the thousands of animals desperate for a loving home? Do remember that owning a pet is a huge responsibility. Every animal needs routine, daily exercise, healthy food … and love. But what you receive in return may be greater than you ever imagined.

"A dog is for life, not just for Easter ..." (Pa Peachey)

"The most important thing for any dog is love." Betty is very wise. She knows exactly how to look after a pet dog. Put up your paw if your dog is as well-looked after as McTavish!

What do dogs need?

1. Love – Most dogs enjoy the company of people they know. Just like you, they want to be part of a loving, friendly home.

2. Training – A well-trained dog is a happy dog. Teach your dog good manners, firmly and with kindness. Start with commands such as "Sit", "Leave" and "Come".

3. Exercise – Dogs need exercise every day, just as you do. When you take your dog to the park, he learns to socialise with different people and pets. Do not let your dog off the lead near traffic or livestock.

4. Play – Does your dog like to chase, grab or pounce when she plays? Try throwing a ball or frisbee, or find a class in agility training. Some breeds need mental activity too, or they become bored and depressed.

5. Good food and fresh water – Dogs need healthy food and clean drinking water. Make sure your dog's diet is right for her age, health and lifestyle. Dogs love treats as a reward – but not too many. Do not overfeed your dog.

6. A 'dog house' – Dogs need their own space. Choose a place for your dog's bed where he can keep an eye on everyone but remain undisturbed.

7. Grooming – Brush or comb your dog at least once a week. Check for lumps and bumps as you groom and contact the vet if you find anything unusual.

8. Health care – Keep your dog in good health by vaccinating him against disease, looking after his teeth, neutering him and by using treatments to prevent worms and fleas.

9. Identification – Put your dog's name and your contact details on a tag on her collar. Your dog must be microchipped too. This is the law in the UK.

10. Well-behaved humans – Stay safe around dogs. Always ask before approaching a strange dog. Never tease, hurt or try to surprise a dog. If a strange dog runs up to you, stand quietly until you are sure he is friendly.

A lovely chicken dinner

"For a miserable moment the entire family stood in the kitchen smelling the delicious smell of poached chicken and rice."

Cook like the Peachey family with this easy-to-follow recipe.

INGREDIENTS

- 2 chicken breasts
- 1 tablespoon soy sauce
- 1 tablespoon olive oil
- Fresh ginger, peeled and grated
- 3 spring onions, sliced
- 175g rice
- 250g mix of broccoli, carrots, green beans, peas (frozen is fine!)
- 400ml chicken or vegetable stock

METHOD

1. Cut the chicken into chunks, mix with the soy sauce and set aside

2. Heat the oil in a pan with a well-fitting lid

3. Fry ginger and onions in the oil – just briefly

4. Rinse the rice under the cold tap, then add to the pan and stir

5. Add the veg and the stock

6. Bring to the boil, reduce the heat, put the lid on and cook for 5 minutes

7. Add the chicken, pour in the soy sauce

8. Stir well, put the lid back on and cook for 15 minutes more till the rice is cooked and everything is tender

9. Serve and enjoy!

About ... Meg Rosoff

Meg Rosoff grew up in Boston, America, and moved to London in 1989. Her first novel, *How I Live Now*, has sold over one million copies in 36 countries. Meg has written seven other novels and her books have won or been shortlisted for 23 international book prizes. In 2016, Meg won the Astrid Lindgren Memorial Award – the world's largest children's literature award – the chair of which said of Meg's work, "Each novel is a little masterpiece." Meg lives in London with her family – and their dogs.

Apparently, Meg has to stop herself visiting the Blue Cross kennels (or worse, the stables), else she'd "end up with 30 rescue dogs, a handful of ponies, a chinchilla and a divorce!"

"No one writes the way Rosoff does ... I love her fizzy honesty, her pluck, her way of untangling emotion through words" *Daily Telegraph*

"Rosoff's writing is luminously beautiful" *Financial Times*

"A voice so stridently pure and direct and funny that you simply can't question it" *Guardian*

About ... McTAVISH

Meg Rosoff says, "I recently met a dog in my local park with a big head, short legs, wearing a tartan coat and with more attitude than any human I'd ever met. His name was McTavish and he clearly needed a book written about him. The real McTavish hasn't met the excellent people at Barrington Stoke yet, but I feel certain he'd love them."

"Warm family drama full of wry humour and a really excellent dog" *The Bookseller*

"Brilliant stuff" *The Bookbag*

COMING SOON ...

"McTavish had made a great deal of progress with the Peachey family since deciding to rescue them, but they still required hard work and patience ..."

What escapades will McTavish and the Peacheys get up to next?

Catch up with them in spring 2018 – when they get tangled up in tents, campfires and all the perils of outdoor life ...